BETTY REN WRIGHT

HAUNTED SUMMER

A
LITTLE
APPLE
PAPERBACK

SCHOLASTIC INC.

New York Toronto London Auckland Sydney
Mexico City New Delhi Hong Kong

ISBN 0-439-24402-1

12 11 10 9 8 7 6 5 4 3 2 1   1 2 3 4 5 6/0

Printed in the U.S.A.   40

First Scholastic paperback printing, July 2001

For George

Contents

Chapter One

Aunt Sarah's Box

"Nothing but clothes," Abby Tolson muttered. She dug deep into the box. "And they'll all be too small!"

Every year Aunt Sarah in Connecticut sent a box full of things that her twin daughters no longer wore. The eleven-year-old twins were a couple of inches shorter and a lot skinnier than Abby, who was nine. Aunt Sarah never remembered that. She just kept sending the boxes, sometimes adding a bracelet or a pin or a bottle of bubble bath her girls didn't want.

Abby's mom shook her head. "Sarah means well," she said. "The twins are just small for their age."

"Or Abby is too big for hers," David commented, without looking up from his book.

"David!" Mrs. Tolson said in a not-one-more-word tone of voice, and Abby flinched. She knew her eleven-year-old brother was teasing, but his words hurt. Big, clumsy, and dumb — that was how he made her feel. Just once she'd like to do something that would make him say, "Hey, not bad! Not bad at all!" But she knew it would never happen.

For a few moments there was silence on the front porch, except for the squeak of David's swing. Then Abby gave a startled "Oh!" She had found something hard buried among the pleats and ruffles in the box.

"Look, Mom!" She pushed the clothes aside and lifted out a little chest of drawers. The chest was white, with blue stars and comet trails painted on the sides. There was a note taped to the top.

Abby, I picked this up at an estate sale. I bought it for the twins, thinking they might like it, but they weren't interested. Hope you can use it, dear.

Carefully, Abby pulled out each of the three little drawers and just as carefully closed them.

"This is the best thing Aunt Sarah ever sent," she said contentedly. "I'm going to keep it forever and ever and put all my jewels in it."

David peered over the top of his book. "You like it but you don't even know what it is, goofy," he said. "There's a key sticking out of the back. That's a music box."

Abby turned the little chest around and, sure enough, there was a key.

"Don't turn it too far," her mom warned. "You might break it."

Abby turned the key once — twice — and waited.

"It's already broken," David said disgustedly. "Why would Aunt Sarah send the poor kid a broken music box? I think that's gross!"

Mrs. Tolson sighed. "I don't *know* why," she said, sounding annoyed. "And please don't call your sister 'poor kid.' Maybe your Aunt Sarah thought Abby would enjoy keeping her jewelry in the drawers. Which is what she plans to do." She reached over and lifted David's book out of his hands. "You can carry the box of clothes into the house, young man. Right now. I'll show you where I want it."

When she was alone, Abby set the music box

next to her on the top step and stared out over
the lawn. She hated not noticing that the chest
was a music box until David told her. She even
hated Aunt Sarah — well, no, not quite, but almost — for sending a *broken* music box. As if
Abby wouldn't know the difference.

A breeze came up, rustling the curtain of
vines that covered one end of the porch. A
cloud drifted across the bright June sun. Abby
picked up the little chest again and thought
about what she would keep in its drawers.
There was the friendship ring her best friend,
Theresa, had given her for her ninth birthday.
And the coral beads Aunt Sarah had sent from
Puerto Rico. And the silver ankle bracelet. She
slid open the top drawer to see how much
room there was, and suddenly, magically, the
music box began to play.

It was a sad and gentle melody that tinkled
out into the warm afternoon. Startled, Abby
closed the drawer. The music stopped. She
opened it, and the tune began again.

So that was it. You had to wind the box first,
then open a drawer to make the music start.
She jumped up, eager to show her mom and
David what she'd figured out. And then, with-

out warning, a gust of wind sent the curtain of vines billowing. A hanging pot of petunias at the top of the steps swung wildly and crashed to the floor. Flowers, dirt, and chunks of pottery showered the top step where Abby had been sitting a second before.

"Mom!" Abby screamed and raced for the door. When she turned and looked out from the safety of the hall, the wind was still blowing. As she stared, her mother's magazine flew the length of the porch.

"Mom!" she screamed again.

The gusting wind sounded wild and angry. It was almost loud enough to drown out the tinkling of the music box in Abby's hands.

Chapter Two

A Face in the Mirror

"This is exactly why we need a sitter for the summer!" Abby's mom exclaimed. She and Abby were sweeping up dirt and bits of pottery. "David thinks because he's eleven, he's old enough to be in charge while we're at work all day, but what if this heavy pot had hit you? You could have been lying here for hours! He'd never know it if he was upstairs reading or working on his butterfly collection."

"I wouldn't *be* upstairs," David retorted from the other side of the screen door. "I would have come down when I heard the crash, Mom." He scowled at the music box that was still pouring out its sad little tune. "For Pete's sake, turn that thing off, Abby. I liked it better when we thought it was broken."

"And that's another thing," Mrs. Tolson said crossly. "Watch your tone, David. Don't bully your sister."

"I don't bully her!"

"You do. I just wish she'd fight back once in a while."

Abby tried not to listen. She didn't want to argue with David. He always won, and she always ended up feeling stupid, even when she was pretty sure she'd been right. She felt the same way at school. It was better to stand back and keep quiet than to speak up and wish she hadn't.

She closed the top drawer of the music box and looked around uneasily. A few minutes ago, when the pot had crashed at her feet, she'd felt as if she were in the middle of a hurricane. But the wind had stopped as quickly as it began, and the sky was blue again. There was nothing to be afraid of, nothing at all.

"We'd be okay alone," she said. She knew that was what David wanted her to say. "I'll be over at Theresa's house part of the time, anyway."

"And Theresa will be here a lot," her mother replied. "That's another reason why there should be an adult in the house. You know, your dad and I will be on the commuter train to the city every morning before you're even out of bed. And we won't get home before six. That's a long time for children to be on their own."

"Hannah Gray isn't even a real adult," David grumbled through the screen. "You said yourself she's only eighteen."

Mrs. Tolson sighed. "No more arguing, please. Hannah has done some baby-sitting in the apartment where she lives and she's a steady, dependable girl. Your father will be bringing her from the Essex station any minute now. I want you to make her feel welcome — is that clear?"

Abby nodded and David scowled. This was the first summer that both of their parents would be working in downtown Chicago for the whole day, and David had been trying to convince them all spring that they didn't need to hire a sitter. Even after Mrs. Tolson announced that she'd found a reliable young lady in the city and had hired her, he refused to give up.

"Maybe she'll be real nice," Abby said hopefully. "Maybe she'll be fun."

"Nice! Fun!" Her brother was scornful. "You can't just have fun all your life."

Why not? Abby wondered, but, as usual, she kept still. David had his whole life planned. He was going to college to study biology. He was going to become a famous scientist. When you were as smart as he was, with straight *A*'s on every report card, you could do anything.

Abby had no idea what she wanted to be when she grew up.

The blast of a horn broke into her thoughts. A moment later the family car swung into the driveway. Abby squinted at the figure in the passenger seat. She waited on the top step while her mother hurried to meet the car.

"Hannah! We're glad you're here. Did you enjoy the train ride?"

"Yes, ma'am."

Hannah Gray's voice was sort of gray, Abby decided, like her name. She was tall and thin, with light-brown hair pulled back into a single braid.

"Well, come right in. This is Abby, and that's David. They've been so anxious to meet you." It was the kind of thing grown-ups always said.

Hannah Gray looked anxiously from Abby to David, as if she didn't believe a word of it.

They all trooped inside and sat down in the living room, except for David who stood just inside the door. "We must get acquainted," Mrs. Tolson said, and Mr. Tolson said, "Right," in a hearty voice. He watched Hannah curiously, as if he couldn't quite figure her out.

"Hannah says this is the first time she's been a live-in sitter," he announced. "In fact, this is the first time she's ever been away from home." He looked at Mrs. Tolson when he said it.

"But she's had lots of experience looking after children in her apartment building," Mrs. Tolson said quickly. "She enjoys children very much."

"Mostly, though, she's home with her aunt, right, Hannah?"

It was a funny way to get acquainted, Abby thought, with her parents doing all the talking. Hannah just sat there, pale and straight, nodding her head at one and then the other.

She's shy, Abby decided, like me. It worried her that a person could be as old as Hannah and still be shy. Abby hoped to outgrow her shyness, the way she kept outgrowing her clothes.

Mr. Tolson leaned forward and cleared his throat. "Well, what do you think, Hannah?" he asked kindly. "Are you going to like being part of our family?"

There was a long pause. "I didn't know you lived so far out in the country," Hannah said, at last, in her flat voice. "And I didn't know it would be such a big house."

David snorted, and Mrs. Tolson shook her head warningly. "You'll get used to all that," she said. "Country living is very pleasant. And you're not expected to clean the house, dear — just enjoy it."

"My friend Theresa Mason lives a little way down Nicholson Road," Abby said. "She's fun. And we have nice pets to keep us company."

"Pets?" Hannah looked startled. "What kind of pets? My aunt and I don't have animals."

"Toby's our dog and our cat is Mister," Abby told her. "They're outside someplace, but they'll be home soon because it's their dinner-time."

Hannah glanced at the front door as if she

expected monsters to crash through the screen and attack her.

"I have other pets, too," David spoke for the first time. His eyes gleamed. "I have — "

"Never mind," Mrs. Tolson interrupted, before he could tell Hannah about the gerbil and the iguana that lived in his bedroom. "I'm sure Hannah would like to see her room now. Abby, you show her where it is, please."

Abby picked up one of Hannah's two suitcases and led the way upstairs. Hannah's room was at the end of the hallway. When they reached it, Hannah sank down on the edge of the bed with a sigh.

"This is all so different," she said softly. "The apartment my aunt and I live in has just four little rooms. And there are lots of people living close by, even though we don't know them very well. And there's traffic noise all day and all night. Your house is so quiet — I can't get used to it. It reminds me of the house where my aunt and I go to séances sometimes. That's big and quiet, too."

"Séances!" Abby was startled. "You mean — like talking to dead people?"

"Sort of." Hannah looked up with a little

frown. "My aunt says it's important to keep in touch with those who have passed on. It's hard to explain. Anyway, the séance house isn't really like yours — it's big, but it's dark and dreary."

"Did you ever see a ghost at a séance?"

Hannah hesitated. "Maybe. . . . Well, I haven't actually *seen* one, but you can *feel* when one is there."

Abby shuddered. She thought it was a good thing Hannah hadn't mentioned the séances when they were getting acquainted downstairs.

"Maybe you'll like being here after you've tried it for a few days," Abby suggested, after a pause. "If you get scared at night, you can tap on the wall of your closet and I'll hear you. My bedroom's right next to yours. Or you can call my mom if you have a bad dream. I do that sometimes."

Hannah nodded, her thin shoulders hunched, her hands clasped. She looked as if she wished she were far away.

Suddenly Abby had an idea. "You wait here, Hannah. I'm going downstairs to get something, but I'll be right back."

When she returned, Hannah hadn't moved.

"I brought you a present," Abby said. "You can put your jewelry in it if you want." She turned the key in the back of the little chest and opened the top drawer. Music spilled out into the room.

For the first time since her arrival, Hannah smiled. She took the music box and carried it to the dressing table. "Thank you very — "

She whirled and stared at the doorway. "Who was that?"

"Who was what?" Abby peered out into the hall. "There's nobody there."

"But there was!" Hannah whispered. "A girl wearing a white cap. I saw her in the mirror. Who was she?"

Abby felt goose bumps pop up on her arms. "You met everybody in our family downstairs," she said. "And there's no one in the hall. Honest!"

"But I *saw* her!" Hannah had a strange, wild-eyed look, as if she were trying not to panic. "A girl in a white cap. She was right there, glaring at us. I don't care if the hall is empty now, Abby. Maybe she's a real person and maybe she's not. But she was there."

Chapter Three

One Scary Summer

As soon as Abby told David about the girl in the white cap, she wished she hadn't.

"Hannah can't help it if she believes in ghosts," she tried to explain. "She knows a lot about them because she goes to séances—" She clapped a hand over her lips, too late.

"*Séances!*" David stared at her as if he could hardly believe his ears. "Oh, boy, what a flake! A sitter who sees ghosts and goes to séances and is scared of *everything*! How did we get so lucky?"

"Don't tell Mom and Dad," Abby begged. "It'll be okay. She'll stop being so nervous after she's lived here for a while."

David looked as if he doubted it, and the next morning Abby wasn't so sure herself.

When she and David came down for breakfast,
their parents had already left for work. Hannah
was standing in a corner with a chair in front
of her, while Toby pranced excitedly around
the kitchen.

"Your dog tried to bite me!" Hannah exclaimed. "He had my whole wrist in his
mouth!"

Abby grabbed Toby's collar and leaned on
his rear to make him sit. "That was just a love
bite," she explained. "Honest, Hannah. He does
that to everybody."

David rolled his eyes.

"Well, I *thought* he was trying to bite me,"
Hannah insisted, pushing the chair away.
"That's just about as frightening."

After breakfast Abby loaded Aunt Sarah's
box of clothes into the old red wagon. "I'm
going to Theresa's house for a while," she said.
"Some of the stuff my aunt sent will fit her."
She hesitated. "I'll take Toby so he won't
bother you. Okay?"

Hannah nodded. "Your mother said you
could go if you wanted to." She looked so uneasy that Abby hated to leave her. It seemed

funny to worry about your sitter, but Hannah
really was a scaredy-cat!

The road shimmered in the bright sun as
Abby trudged along. Toby trotted beside the
wagon, tugging on his leash at times to chase
a grasshopper into the tall grass. As they
walked, Abby's spirits rose with every step.
This was going to be a good summer.

But when she turned in at Theresa's driveway, she knew right away that something was
wrong. The Masons' van was parked at the side
of the house. Boxes and suitcases and bedrolls
were stacked next to it. As Abby stared, puzzled, the front door of the house burst open.
Theresa raced across the yard, her long blond
hair flying.

"We're going!" she shouted. "We're going to
the wedding!"

"What wedding?" Abby dragged Toby away
from the open door of the van.

"You know," Theresa said impatiently. "I
told you my aunt is getting married out in Oregon, and my dad said we couldn't afford to
go, but now he's changed his mind. If we leave
today, we can just make it. And when the wed-

ding's over we're going camping — in the *mountains*! We'll be gone three whole weeks!" She spun around and stopped in front of the wagon. "Is that a box from your aunt Sarah?"

Abby nodded and bent over the box. Three weeks! That was a long time. All at once the day lost its sparkle.

"There's a blue dress with a ruffled skirt in here," she said. "Maybe you can wear it to the wedding."

As usual, it turned out that most of the clothes in Aunt Sarah's box fit Theresa perfectly. Abby felt *clunky*, standing around while her friend tried on dresses and skirts and pants, and folded some of them into her suitcase. Watching a person pack was boring — and painful — if you weren't going along.

"I'd better go home," she said after a while. "Our new sitter and I are going to play games and stuff."

Theresa looked startled, as if she'd just remembered all the things she and Abby had planned to do, starting today. "We'll have fun when I get back," she promised. "It'll just be three weeks."

Three weeks. Twenty-one days. Three Mondays, three Tuesdays. . . . On the way home, Abby tried different ways of saying it. Every way sounded long. Hannah was right: Living in the country was lonely.

When she reached her driveway, she saw the sitter crouched on the front porch steps, her drab cotton skirt pulled tight over her knees.

"I didn't think you'd be back this soon," Hannah said, sounding relieved. Abby put Toby in the house and returned to the porch. "I thought you'd spend the day with your friend."

"She's going away."

"Oh, I'm sorry." Hannah sounded as if she meant it. "Where's she going?"

"Oregon." Abby didn't want to talk.

"You'll miss each other," Hannah said, but Abby shook her head.

"No, we won't. At least Theresa won't miss me. She's glad she's going."

Hannah started to say something and stopped. She stood up quickly and smoothed her skirt. "It's lunchtime. Do you like grilled cheese sandwiches? My aunt says I make good ones."

Abby loved them, but she felt too grumpy to say so. "They're okay, I guess."

Hannah opened the door and led the way inside. Then she stopped, so suddenly that Abby bumped into her.

"Listen! It's the music box you gave me. It's playing — upstairs — all by itself!"

Abby gulped. "It can't be," she said. "You have to open a drawer — " She stopped. The music box *was* playing. "Maybe David — "

"He's in that field behind the garage looking for bugs," Hannah said in her flat voice. "Let's go back outside."

Abby wondered if they were going to spend the entire summer sitting on the porch steps. Instead of following Hannah, she started up the stairs.

"Abby, you mustn't!" Hannah sounded as if she were going to cry.

Abby hesitated and then kept going. She wasn't afraid of the music box. By the time she reached the top of the stairs, Hannah caught up with her. Together they tiptoed down the hall toward Hannah's bedroom.

When they reached the last doorway, Abby

took a deep breath and peeked inside. The music box lay on its side on the dressing table with one drawer partly open. Tinkling music filled the room.

"It just fell over, see?" Abby hurried to close the drawer and set the box upright, while Hannah hesitated at the door.

"It couldn't fall over all by itself," she protested. "It couldn't!"

Just then something black streaked out of the closet and disappeared under the dresser. Hannah screamed and leaped onto the bed.

"What was that?" She huddled on her knees, clutching a pillow in front of her.

"That was Mister," Abby said, giggling with relief. "He's a really nosy cat. You'll have to keep your bedroom door shut if you don't want him to come visiting."

Hannah dropped the pillow. "You mean it was the cat who knocked over the box?" She giggled, too. "Oh, my! If your mother finds out how frightened I was — "

"I won't tell," Abby promised. "I was scared, too."

"But you came upstairs anyway," Hannah

reminded her. She followed Abby out into the hall and closed the bedroom door firmly behind her. "You're braver than I am."

Abby went down the stairs two at a time. She wouldn't tell her mom and dad that Hannah was afraid of just about everything. And she wouldn't tell *anyone* that for a second — no, just part of a second — she'd imagined a flash of white in the dressing table mirror, as if something had moved out of sight in the hall, behind Hannah.

It hadn't happened; she knew that. But when she thought about it, she didn't feel brave at all. This was starting to be one scary summer.

Chapter Four

There's Someone Up There!

"Hannah's the biggest coward I've ever met!" David muttered. He and Abby were hosing down their bikes and polishing the chrome. "I put Rex out in the hall so he could get some exercise, and you should have heard her scream!"

"You scared her on purpose," Abby said. Rex was David's iguana, twenty-two inches long and looking more like a dragon every day. Of course Hannah had been frightened when she saw him! "You want to make her quit. You don't like her."

"Liking has nothing to do with it," David growled. "We don't need a sitter, that's all. And we especially don't need *her*. She's not even very bright — that stuff about seeing a ghost

23

is crazy! What if we had a *real* problem? She'd scream and hide, that's what!"

Abby bit her lip. David was so sure about everything. And it was true that Hannah was a timid person. If a burglar broke in, she *might* be too frightened to move. I would be, too, Abby thought. I'd just stand there like a big dummy. David would be the one who called the sheriff.

"Well, I don't think you should pick on her," Abby said. "She can't help it if she's nervous." She promised herself that she'd stay close to Hannah for a while, in case David was planning more surprises.

But she couldn't stand guard every minute. The next afternoon Hannah dashed downstairs, wide-eyed and pale. "Somebody's in the attic!" she exclaimed. "I heard footsteps over my room."

Abby looked out the window. David had gone past the living room with his butterfly net a while ago.

"It wasn't David," Hannah said quickly, following her glance. "He said he wouldn't be back for a couple of hours. Besides, why would he be prowling in the attic?"

Abby didn't answer. Maybe her brother had figured out a new way to frighten Hannah. Or, maybe the sitter was imagining things again.

Once more, she and Hannah tiptoed upstairs. Hannah opened the door at the foot of the attic steps.

"We'd better not go any farther," she whispered. "If the girl is there . . ."

Abby didn't ask what girl. There wasn't a sound from the attic. Not a squeak. Specks of dust floated in the sunlight at the top of the stairs.

"We'll just take one quick look," she coaxed. "If someone's there, we'll run."

Hannah sighed but gave in. Hand in hand they went up the stairs, stopping two steps from the top to look around. As Abby had expected, the attic was empty, except for boxes piled against the walls on either side. A breeze drifted through the gable window.

"The window's open." Abby pointed. "Maybe a squirrel came in to look around and went out again." She hurried across the room and closed the window. "There! Now he can't come back."

"Oh, it wasn't a squirrel, Abby." Hannah

peered anxiously into the corners. "It was a person walking around. I heard her!"

The following morning Hannah hardly spoke as she and Abby and David ate breakfast. Her hands shook when she buttered her toast.

"Let's go for a hike," Abby suggested. It was what she and Theresa would be doing, if Theresa weren't on her way to Oregon.

Hannah agreed at once, as if she were ready to do anything to get out of the house. To Abby's surprise, she turned out to be a good hiking companion. Even though she was a city person, she'd read a lot about trees and wildflowers. She liked birds, too, and could name many of them. And though she still drew away when Toby bounced between them, she wasn't as afraid of him as she had been. On the way home she actually threw a stick for him to fetch.

That afternoon they played Monopoly. It would have been easier at the kitchen table, but Hannah suggested a card table on the front porch. They had fun, even though the money kept blowing away.

"You're a good player," Hannah said after a while. "You spend your money wisely."

Abby was surprised and pleased. David had often said it was dull playing with her, because she never took chances.

The next morning, as soon as breakfast was over, Hannah suggested they take another hike.

"Not *every* day," Abby protested. She tried to think of something she and Hannah could do on the porch. Suddenly she remembered a project she and Theresa had started, but not finished, last summer.

"Let's make a shoe box house," she suggested. "You make furniture out of cardboard and scraps of cloth and fix up rooms in shoe boxes," she explained, when Hannah looked puzzled. "There's a bunch of shoe boxes in the basement, and I've got a box of things Theresa and I made. I'll get them." She hurried down to the basement without waiting for Hannah to agree.

When she returned, Hannah had set up the card table and two folding chairs in the backyard. "David's reading on the porch," she explained. "We won't bother him out here."

They worked on the shoe box house for the rest of the day, stopping only for a quick lunch of peanut butter sandwiches. Abby had forgotten how much she liked cutting and pasting.

"And you're really good at it!" Hannah said admiringly. "That little bed is just perfect." She picked up a scrap of white silk and stitched busily, while Abby cut and folded a piece of cardboard to make a bureau and then drew drawers on the front. By the time the bureau was completed, Hannah was fitting a bed-spread on the cardboard bed.

"We make a good team," Hannah said with a little smile. "Let's do this again tomorrow. Out here."

That evening Mr. Tolson sat out on the porch with Abby and David while Hannah helped to prepare dinner.

"How are things going with Hannah?" he asked. "She seems so jumpy — I can't think what's wrong with the girl."

"She's a big baby, that's what!" David told him. "She's scared of her own shadow."

"What do *you* say, Abby?"

Abby squirmed. She didn't look at her brother. "I think she's nice," she said softly. "We have good times together. She's getting used to being here."

But Thursday morning Hannah announced at breakfast that she'd heard footsteps in the attic again, and on Friday she was so quiet that Abby gave up trying to talk to her. Instead, she followed David when he went out to the meadow with his butterfly net.

"Hannah's going to quit," he said confidently, as soon as they were out of the yard. "Wait and see. Tonight she goes home for the weekend, and I bet she won't come back. If she doesn't quit, she's going to tell Mom and Dad our house is haunted, and they'll fire her."

"That's not fair!" Abby protested. "You want her to be afraid. I bet you're the one who's scaring her." She paused, hoping he would say it wasn't true, but he just grinned.

"Is it my fault she can't take a joke?"

A joke? What was he talking about? Abby started to ask, but David cut her off. "Now look what you've done! That was an American Copper on that milkweed, and you scared it away. Go away! I can't catch anything while you're clomping around here."

Abby sighed and turned back to the house. For the first time, she noticed that one big branch of the oak tree curved close to the

attic window. David was a terrific climber.
If he sneaked upstairs and opened the attic window before breakfast, he could have
climbed the tree later and walked around
the attic while Hannah and Abby thought he
was butterfly hunting. He might have been
perched up there in the branches, chuckling to
himself, while they searched the attic for the
burglar.

Maybe, maybe not. Even if it were true, Abby
didn't know what to do about it. She liked Hannah and was glad to have her company. But
David wouldn't be satisfied until the sitter was
gone, and maybe Hannah would be happier
then, too. She certainly didn't seem to be enjoying her job.

"I hope he doesn't go too far!"

Abby jumped. She hadn't seen Hannah come
around the corner of the house.

"It's going to rain," Hannah went on, looking
uneasy. "The radio says there's a big storm
coming this way. David will get soaked — just
look at that sky!"

"He won't care if he does," Abby assured
her. "We like storms." She wondered if Hannah
was afraid of thunder, too.

With dragging feet she followed the sitter into the house. She was tired of worrying. Most of all, she was tired of being caught in the middle, with her determined brother on one side and scaredy-cat Hannah on the other.

Chapter Five

Hiding From a Ghost

It was nearly noon before the storm finally arrived. Abby and Hannah were working on shoe box furniture at the kitchen table, and David had retreated to his bedroom, taking Toby with him. All at once, rain battered the windows and wind rattled the panes. Abby's scissors slipped, snipping off the leg of the cardboard table she was building.

The ceiling light in the kitchen flickered and went out.

"Oh, no!" Hannah leaped up, almost knocking over her chair. She ran to the foot of the stairs in the front hall. "David, come down here, please."

For a moment there was no answer. Then a shout made Abby race to Hannah's side.

"Who's there?"

A flurry of footsteps sounded in the upstairs hall, followed by barking. David hurtled down the steps with Toby behind him.

"There's somebody up there!" he puffed. "A girl! I saw her!"

He was trying to look scared, but Abby knew him too well to be fooled.

"Don't say that!" she begged. "Don't make up any more stories, okay? There isn't any girl!"

"Hey, I'm telling you I saw her." David pointed up the stairs. "She was right up there — a girl in a white cap. She sort of floated down the hall to Hannah's bedroom. And then she disappeared."

"Go into the kitchen!" Hannah cried. "Hurry!" She pushed Abby ahead of her down the hall and dragged David along by one wrist. Toby scooted between them as thunder crashed close by.

Back in the kitchen, Hannah slammed the door behind them. "Come on, help me!" She pulled chairs out of the way and shoved the

table against the hall door. Then she closed the
door to the dining room and wedged a chair
under the knob.

"We're going to stay right here until your
mother and father come home," she announced shakily. "Right here! Doors don't keep
her out, but as long as we stay together ... I
can't think what else to do." She sank into a
chair and covered her face with her hands.
"When your parents come, you can tell them
what you saw up there, David."

David scowled, and Abby knew what he was
thinking. His story about a girl in a white cap
would get him into big trouble. Scaring Hannah
was one thing; convincing his parents he'd actually seen a ghost was another.

"Maybe I didn't see anyone," he muttered.
"The hall was pretty dark, you know. It could
have been a lightning flash — or something. I
think I imagined it — that could happen."

"No!" Hannah sounded close to tears. "I've
seen her. I've heard her. And I know she'll hurt
us if she can!"

"Mom and Dad will never believe David saw
a ghost," Abby told her. "They'll be angry."
Angry with you, too, she added silently. Han-

nah was her friend, and she didn't want to lose her.

She went to the window and looked out. The branches of the oak tree danced in the wind, and the meadow grass rippled in waves. Usually Abby enjoyed thunderstorms, but this one was different. The dark kitchen, the furniture pushed against the doors, the way Hannah was sitting, hunched over and clenching her hands as if she might fly apart at any moment — all of those things together made Abby wish she were somewhere else. Oregon, maybe. Camping with Theresa and her family.

"This is really dumb," David grumbled. "I'm going back upstairs."

"No," Hannah said. "You mustn't. I'm afraid of what the girl might do." She didn't raise her voice, but there was something in her tone that kept David from moving the table away from the door.

The minutes passed slowly. It was nearly an hour before the wind died and the thunder finally moved off into the distance.

"There's a rainbow!" Abby pointed at the sky above the meadow. Hannah came to the window to look, and as they stood there the kitchen light came back on. The refrigerator began to hum.

"*Now* can we get out of here?" David demanded. "I've got stuff to do."

"When your folks get home," Hannah insisted. "It won't be long."

"Well, I'm *not* going to tell them about the girl." David's self-confidence seemed to have returned with the end of the storm. "They'd never believe there was a ghost — and they won't like it if they know *you* believe it," he added triumphantly.

"They really won't, Hannah," Abby said anxiously. "Can't we just not talk about it?"

Hannah watched the rainbow for another minute, and then, as it began to fade, she turned away from the window.

"I suppose you're right," she said slowly. "We'll open the doors, but please, *please* stay downstairs until your parents come home. You don't have to tell them what you saw if you don't want to, David. It's up to you. I — I don't know what to do."

"We can make pizzas," Abby suggested. She was pleased when Hannah agreed, even though she knew that supper wasn't what Hannah meant when she said she didn't know what to do.

Two hours later, Mr. Tolson drove away toward Essex and the railroad station with Hannah sitting stiffly beside him. Abby waved until the car was out of sight. Then she sank down on the porch steps with a sigh.

"What's the matter, hon?" her mom wanted to know. "Are you going to miss Hannah this weekend? I think she's pretty homesick — she hardly spoke during supper. But she'll be back soon."

"Maybe not," David muttered, from the other end of the porch. "Maybe she won't be back at all."

Mrs. Tolson looked startled. "Whatever makes you say that?" she asked sharply. "Did she tell you she isn't happy here?"

"Not exactly." David hid behind his magazine, but Abby knew he was smiling. "I just have this feeling."

Mrs. Tolson groaned. "That's all I need to hear at the end of a hard week," she murmured. "I certainly hope your feeling is wrong."

"I hope so, too," Abby said. But Hannah

had said she was going to have to make up
her mind what to do next. Judging from the
look on her face as she was driven away,
Abby was pretty sure she had already decided.

Chapter Six

"I Heard the Music Box!"

Saturday afternoon Abby and her mom went to Essex to buy groceries for the week. When they returned, the men in the family were sitting on the front porch. Myrtle the gerbil and Rex the iguana were there, too, enjoying the sunshine.

Abby reached into Myrtle's box and stroked her twitchy nose.

"David says he can't let the animals out of his room when Hannah's around," Mr. Tolson commented from the swing. "He says she had hysterics when she saw Rex."

"I'm not especially fond of him myself," Mrs. Tolson retorted. "Come on, Abby. Help me put the food away."

Abby saw the look that passed between her

mom and dad. Her father was convinced that Hannah was too timid to be a good sitter. Her mother didn't want to talk about it. Abby was grateful, all over again, that they didn't know she and David and Hannah had spent yesterday afternoon hiding from a ghost.

Saturday evening was fun. They had macaroni and cheese for supper and chocolate sundaes for dessert. They were Abby's favorite foods in all the world. Afterward, they watched a funny movie her father had brought home from the city.

"That was neat," Abby said with a contented sigh when the movie ended. "I wish Hannah could have seen it." She'd been thinking about Hannah all evening, hoping she was having a good time at home and wondering if she was going to come back.

David made a face. "Hannah wouldn't like it," he said. "The millionaire's house was too big. His dog was too big. She'd be afraid to watch."

"That's enough!" Mrs. Tolson interrupted. "I hope you aren't this unpleasant when Hannah's in charge, David. No wonder she was glad to go home for the weekend."

"I'm not unpleasant," David protested. "I'm just telling you we don't need a sitter. Especially one who's afraid of the whole world."

"But I don't understand what it is she's afraid of," Mr. Tolson complained. "Besides Rex, that is."

David shrugged. "Everything," he muttered and shot a warning glance at Abby.

"She's not afraid of Myrtle," Abby said. "I mean, she wouldn't be, if she'd ever seen her."

"Well, I should hope not," her father said. "Deliver me from screamers."

"Me, too," David said. "Who needs 'em!"

That night Abby had a weird dream. She was in the toy shop near the railroad station in Essex, walking past shelves of stuffed animals, when she heard a movement behind her. She whirled around and discovered a huge stuffed lion creeping up the aisle. Then every toy in the store began to move. A car scooted between her feet. Music tinkled from a little piano at the end of the aisle. Its keys bobbed up and down, and the music grew louder . . . LOUDER!

She woke up stiff with fright. Across the moonlit room her favorite stuffed animals crouched on the window seat. They weren't

moving. It was only in dreams that stuffed animals came to life and toy pianos played by
themselves. . . .

But she could still hear the music! She
gasped and pulled the bedsheet up to her chin.
That gentle, tinkling tune wasn't the sound of
a toy piano. It was Aunt Sarah's music box.

For a few seconds Abby lay still, listening
for footsteps in the hall. Surely her mom and
dad, or David, would hear the music, too, and
would come to investigate. But the house was
silent except for the eerie music.

Mister! she thought, and she let out the
breath she'd been holding. Maybe the cat had
slipped into Hannah's room and knocked over
the music box again.

She pushed back the covers and tiptoed out
into the hall. Hannah's door was tightly closed.
Could Mister have been accidentally trapped
inside? She paused, trying to decide what to
do. Then, with shaking fingers she turned the
doorknob and pushed. She slid one hand
through the opening and flicked the light
switch.

The music stopped.

In the silence that followed, she opened the

door a little farther and stepped inside. The room was primly neat, the way Hannah was neat. The hairbrush and comb and fingernail file that Hannah kept in a row on the dressing table were gone.

"What're you doing, dopey? Walking in your sleep?"

David's whisper from the hall behind her was so unexpected that Abby squeaked in fright.

"You scared me!" she gasped, when she'd caught her breath. "I — I heard the music box!"

"What music box?"

Abby pointed toward the dressing table and frowned. The music box was gone, too.

"The music box Aunt Sarah sent," she whispered. "I gave it to Hannah. I heard it playing just now, but — but I don't know where it is."

"She took it home with her, of course. I told you, she's not coming back." David tiptoed across the room and opened the closet door. One skirt and two blouses hung there. A pair of shoes and a suitcase were on the floor. "She'll ask Mom to send the rest of her stuff later, you'll see."

"But the music box — "

"It's not here, can't you see?" David was impatient. "You just thought you heard it. Boy, you're getting as bad as Hannah!"

"Hannah and I aren't the only ones who are scared," Abby said. "You *said* you saw a ghost Friday afternoon."

David yawned. "You know I made that up, dopey. There wasn't any ghost then, and there wasn't any music now. So quit prowling around and go back to sleep, okay?"

Abby gave up. It was easier than arguing. But she knew she wasn't going to be able to sleep any more that night. She *knew* she had heard the music box. And when she'd stepped inside Hannah's bedroom, there'd been a moment when she'd *felt* someone there, the way Hannah had said she could feel the presence of a ghost at a séance.

That was true, even if David would never believe it.

Chapter Seven

"Hannah's My Friend!"

Sunday evening Abby rode into Essex with her dad to meet the train.

"You're wasting your time," David had told them smugly. "She isn't coming back."

Mrs. Tolson had shaken her head at him. "Hannah is a dependable person. She would have called if she weren't coming."

"She might not," David had argued. "She might be afraid you'd be mad. If I know Hannah, she'll write to you in a couple of days and ask you to send her things. And that'll be that."

Abby had wanted to tell him that he *didn't* know Hannah at all. Hannah was good and kind. She was fun to be with when she wasn't afraid. Being timid was like being too big for your age. Some people looked at you and that was all they saw.

"Well, we'll soon know whether David's right," Mr. Tolson said as they drove into town. "If Hannah's not on the train I guess we'll have to call Grandma Tolson and see if she can come for a few days, until we find someone else."

"David won't like that."

Her father shrugged. "You're probably right."

Grandma Tolson took a nap every afternoon and expected other people to do the same. She didn't approve of peanut butter or chocolate cake or iguanas. She wasn't afraid of iguanas, she just didn't approve of them.

The shrill wail of the diesel sounded as they turned into the station parking lot. By the time Abby reached the platform, the train was screeching to a stop.

Hannah was the first person to step off.

"Hi!" Abby darted forward and hugged Hannah around the waist.

"Obviously, we're happy to see you," Mr. Tolson said with a grin. He picked up Hannah's suitcase. "We were afraid you might have decided to stay in the big city."

Hannah looked startled. "Oh, I couldn't do

that," she told him seriously. "I had to come back."

"Well, we're glad you did." Mr. Tolson put the suitcase into the car trunk, while Abby and Hannah climbed into the front seat. On the way home Mr. Tolson and Hannah talked about how crowded the train had been and about the weather. Abby sat between them, wondering if Hannah had brought the music box back in her suitcase.

As they turned onto Nicholson Road, Hannah stopped talking. She sat very straight. Her hands were clenched in her lap and her jaw was set. Abby thought she looked like a person who was going to the dentist.

Mr. Tolson glanced at her curiously. "Is there anything we can do to make your stay with us more pleasant, Hannah?" he asked as they swung into the driveway. "Is David giving you a hard time? I can talk to him. . . ."

"Oh, David's fine," Hannah said earnestly. "And Abby — Abby is wonderful."

Mr. Tolson chuckled. "Look at her blush," he teased.

Abby didn't mind the teasing. *Abby is wonderful.* It was a moment to enjoy, made even better by the look on her brother's face as Hannah stepped out of the car.

Before she went to bed that night, and again the next morning, Abby peeked into Hannah's room. The brush and comb and fingernail file were back on the dressing table, but the little white chest of drawers was not.

When she went downstairs, Hannah was busy making sandwiches in the kitchen, while David stood at the window, his shoulders hunched.

"We're going for another hike today," Hannah announced. "Your mother thinks we all need more exercise, and so do I. She said there's a nice pond about a mile from here where we can have lunch."

"Perkins Pond," Abby said. "It's really pretty."

"Well, I'm not going," David snapped. "I get plenty of exercise. Who cares about a pond?"

"We do." Hannah sounded determined. "And your mother said you're to go, too, David. You can catch butterflies."

"I can do that by myself," David grumped. "You'd scare them away."

Hannah didn't say anything more, and it wasn't clear to Abby who had won the argument. But when the breakfast table was cleared, Hannah took the house keys from the nail behind the door and handed David the picnic basket.

"All set?" She opened the back door. "Let's go."

Abby hurried out to the back porch, and a moment later David followed, scowling fiercely. Toby came, too, prancing with excitement.

"Lead the way, Abby," Hannah said. "We'll be right behind you."

Abby waded into the tall grass beyond the garage. Each time she glanced back, Hannah appeared a little more cheerful, as if she were leaving her troubles behind her. Abby couldn't see David's face, but she could hear him. He kept yawning noisily, to make it clear how bored he was.

When they reached the edge of the woods, Hannah stopped.

"Do you know what you sound like, David?" She waited, but he didn't answer. "You sound like the oldest lion at the Brookfield Zoo. His

name is Oscar, and all day long he lies in the
sun and yawns — like this." She opened her
mouth very wide and made a huge sound, halfway between a yawn and a growl. It was so
unlike Hannah that Abby laughed out loud and
David's lips twitched in a grin. He shrugged, as
if he didn't care that he sounded like a lazy
lion, but Abby noticed that he didn't yawn
again.

Still, she knew her brother hadn't forgiven
Hannah for making him come with them. When
they reached Perkins Pond, he wandered down
to the water's edge and stayed there while Hannah and Abby tossed a Frisbee and Toby
dashed back and forth between them.

"This is perfect," Hannah said, when they
tired of the game at last and settled down on
the grass. Her thin face, so pale and tense back
at the house, was pink and cheerful in the sunlight.

Abby unpacked the picnic basket. They had
finished their first sandwich and started on seconds before David returned. He helped himself
to a sandwich and sat down on a stump. A
moment later, a frog hopped into Hannah's lap.

"Oh!" Hannah opened her mouth to scream and then didn't. With a fingertip she edged the frog off her lap and into the grass.

"I guess the poor thing has more right to be here than we have," she said, and she looked David squarely in the eyes. "It's not like finding a giant lizard in the hall outside your bedroom door," she added. "That *did* scare me."

David turned away. "Iguanas are just as nice as frogs," he muttered. "Nicer!"

After lunch they followed the path around the pond. The water was a clear pale brown, like iced tea, and the sun was hot. When the path skimmed the very edge of the water, Abby kicked off her sneakers and waded in. Hannah followed her.

"Baby stuff," David muttered. He grabbed Toby's collar and kept on walking. They caught sight of him once in a while through the trees.

"Don't worry," Hannah said, when she saw Abby's troubled expression. "David is all right. He just likes to tease."

"But he shouldn't try to scare you," Abby said. "It's not nice."

Hannah wiggled her toes in the cool water.

"Don't worry," she repeated. "We're having a good time today, aren't we? Nothing can spoil it."

But something did. When they returned to the spot where they'd left the lunch bag, David was waiting for them.

"Did you see her?" he asked innocently. "That girl with the white cap?"

Hannah stared. "You saw her — here?"

"I think so." David acted as if it didn't matter whether they believed him or not. "When I was on the other side of the pond, I looked across and I thought I saw her watching you in the water."

"You're making that up!" Abby exclaimed. "I know it!"

"I said I wasn't sure."

Hannah's lips were set in a tight line. She bent and gathered up the soda cans lying next to the basket.

"Time we started back, anyway," she said unhappily.

"It's early," Abby protested. "Mom and Dad won't be home till six o'clock." But she knew it was no use. Just the mention of the girl in the white cap was enough to upset Hannah,

even when it was perfectly clear that David
was fibbing.

When they reached home, Abby stayed in the
kitchen while Hannah started dinner. David
went upstairs for a book. By the time he returned, Abby had made up her mind. She followed him out to the porch and took a deep
breath.

"If you keep trying to scare Hannah, I'm
going to tell Mom and Dad," she said. "You're
being mean!"

David snorted. "Tattletale. What's it to you?"

"Hannah's my friend!" Abby told him. "I want
her to stay, even if you don't."

"If you tell," David said, "Mom and Dad will
just think Hannah was stupid to believe me.
Anyway, I didn't say I saw the girl for sure. I
said I *might* have seen her. It's up to Hannah
if she wants to make a big deal of it. If I told
her the music box was playing when I went
upstairs just now, she'd probably faint."

"It wasn't!" Abby grabbed his arm. "You're
making that up, too! The music box isn't even
here. I looked this morning."

"I'm *not* making it up," David retorted. "It's

up there somewhere. I heard it as clear as anything — just for a minute, and then it stopped.
Maybe it was wound too tight. Now go away
and let me read. Quit being a big baby."

Hannah was in the hall when Abby entered
the house.

"I heard him," she said tiredly. "What he said
about the music box. And this time he was
probably telling the truth."

"No, he wasn't!" Abby exclaimed. "He
couldn't have heard it. You took the music box
home with you, didn't you?"

Hannah shook her head. "It's been right here
all the time." She rubbed her forehead as if it
ached. "Abby, I'm almost sure there's some
connection between the music box and the girl
in the white cap. Ever since that first day —
when you gave me the box — I've felt that girl
reaching out for it. I've seen her! Last week I
hid it under some blankets on the top shelf of
my closet, and it's there now. But hiding it
doesn't help. She can make it play whenever
she wants to. If David heard it, then that girl
is in the house this very minute!"

Chapter Eight

Abby Tolson, Detective

The next day Abby did a very un-Abbylike thing. Without asking anyone if it was all right, she called Aunt Sarah in Connecticut.

"Abby? Is that really you? Is anything wrong, dear?" Her aunt's voice was cool and a little impatient.

"I — I'm okay," Abby stammered. "Everybody's okay here, Aunt Sarah. I just thought I'd call you. To thank you for the things you sent — especially the music box."

"Music box?" Aunt Sarah sounded puzzled. "Oh, that. I'm glad you liked it, Abby. I thought it was sweet. I bought it because I thought the twins might like a souvenir of Essex, Wisconsin, where their mother — and yours — grew up, but as usual, I was wrong. They couldn't have cared less. So I decided to send it back to Wisconsin, where it belonged."

Startled, Abby forgot her shyness. "You mean the music box came from Essex? Our Essex?"

"That's right. I think I told you I found it at an estate sale. It belonged to a wealthy old couple called Erlandson who moved from Wisconsin to Connecticut about fifteen years ago to be near their only daughter. After they died, the daughter sold most of their things, and I bought the music box. Their daughter said it was one of the few items they'd brought from their old home."

The music box came from Essex! Abby wondered if that was important. She decided it must be.

"Is there anything else, dear? If not, I have to pick up the girls after their riding lesson in about ten minutes. Does your mother know you're calling?"

"No," Abby admitted. "But I'm going to pay for the call out of my allowance. I just wanted to talk to you."

"Oh." Aunt Sarah sounded more puzzled

than ever. "Well, that's very nice, Abby. I'm flattered. Good-bye, dear."

"Bye."

Abby put down the phone and ran out to the front porch where Hannah and David were reading. Excitedly, she told them what she'd learned.

"Big deal," David commented. "What's so important about that old music box, anyway? You're going to be in trouble for making a long-distance call without asking."

"Hannah thinks" — Abby glanced at Hannah, who was listening intently — "Hannah thinks the ghost in the white cap is haunting us because of the music box."

David groaned. "Don't be dumb! There isn't any ghost."

"Hannah's seen her," Abby protested. "She saw her the very first night she was here. And you — "

"I *never* saw her." David turned to Hannah defiantly. "I made all that up. It was a joke!"

"I know." Hannah didn't seem surprised. "I believed you the first time," she added. "But yesterday I was sure you were just pretending.

It doesn't matter. There really *is* a girl in a
white cap, David. I didn't want to frighten you
and Abby, but *she's come to my room almost
every night since I've been here.* Sometimes
the music box starts to play by itself, and then
I know she's nearby. She listens for a while,
and then she turns around and stares at me
with so much hatred, I can hardly bear it. Last
week I hid the box in the closet before I left,
hoping she'd think it was gone. But it plays
anyway — and she comes."

Abby shuddered. No wonder Hannah acted
scared all the time!

"Now you're the one who's making up stories," David blustered. "There's no such thing
as a ghost."

"When she comes, I can feel her anger all
around me," Hannah said solemnly. "It's hor-
rible! I'm so afraid of what she might do."

"Like what?" Abby asked shakily. "What
might she do?"

"I don't know," Hannah admitted. "More
than anything, I'd like to tell your mother and
father what's happening, but I know they
wouldn't believe me. I thought about taking the
music box home with me and leaving it there,

but I was afraid that would only make the girl angrier."

And that's why you came back on Sunday, Abby thought. You were worried about what might happen to us. Oh, Hannah, you really are our friend!

David's face was pale. "That's crazy talk!" he exclaimed. "You don't scare me. I don't believe in spooks."

"I know," Hannah told him, not sounding angry at all. "You don't have to believe if you don't want to. But I've seen her, David. I have to believe."

Halfway through the pot roast and potatoes that night, Abby had an idea.

"Would it be all right if we rode into town with you tomorrow morning?" she asked her mom. "We could go to the library and have lunch someplace and then take the bus home."

"If Hannah wants to," Mrs. Tolson said. "And you can get up early enough."

Hannah looked at Abby thoughtfully. "That would be nice."

"Not me — " David began, but his mom interrupted.

"All of you, then. You can use a change."

"I don't need a change," David protested. But he stopped arguing when his dad suggested that if he stayed home he could clean the basement.

Abby stayed awake for a long time that night. She didn't know what she expected to learn in Essex, but she hoped they could find out something about the music box. Maybe Hannah would have some ideas.

It was scary, thinking of Hannah — her friend — in the next room, wide-awake, too, and waiting for the ghost-girl to appear. Once, close to midnight, Abby thought she heard the music box playing, but she couldn't be sure.

The next thing she knew, it was morning, and Toby was licking her face to wake her.

"Time to get up," Hannah said from the doorway. "Your folks are already eating breakfast." She looked as tired as Abby felt.

"There's a pretty tearoom in town where you can have lunch," Mrs. Tolson said as they settled themselves in the car a half hour later. "And besides the library, there's the park and some nice little shops."

David groaned.

"We'll find plenty to do," Hannah assured her. She smiled at Abby, as if they were partners, but she didn't say anything more until the train pulled away from the station.

"Now," she exclaimed, "let's go over to that phone booth! I've been trying to figure out how we can learn something about the music box and the people who owned it — and I think I have an idea!"

Abby followed her excitedly. David lagged behind as usual, grumbling. After a quick check of the phone book, Hannah jotted a number on a scrap of paper and handed it to Abby.

"You're the detective, Abby — you do the calling. This is the number of the Essex Home for the Elderly. Ask if there's anyone living there named Erlandson — maybe a relative of the Mr. and Mrs. Erlandson who moved to Connecticut fifteen years ago — or maybe a friend who knew them well. Just say you'd like to talk to someone who might have known them."

"They won't pay any attention to a kid," David said. "And she'll get it all wrong."

Abby winced. "You do it, Hannah."

But Hannah shook her head. "Try," she urged.

The woman who answered Abby's call sounded brisk and hurried, a little like Aunt Sarah.

"There are no Erlandsons here," she announced. But then, as Abby was about to hang up, the voice softened. "We do have one resident who might be able to help you. And I know he would enjoy company. His name is Leonard Bonner, and I believe he worked as a gardener for a lot of people in Essex when he was younger. Did these Erlandsons have a garden?"

"I don't know," Abby said timidly. "But I think they lived in a big house."

"Well, then. You talk to Leonard. If he didn't know the people you're looking for, he might be able to tell you someone else who can help."

Abby hung up and reported what the woman had said. She was careful not to look at David, who would surely say she hadn't learned anything at all.

"Good work!" Hannah said. "Now, how do we get to this Mr. Bonner? Is it too far to walk?"

"Six blocks." David sounded bored. "The home's way at the other end of Main Street."

"Let's go."

The sun was hot, and they were all dragging their feet by the time they reached the spread of lawn in front of the Essex Home for the Elderly. David slumped in a chair just inside the door. Abby and Hannah went up to the woman seated at a desk.

"Are you the young lady who wants to meet Len Bonner?" the woman asked cheerfully. "He's probably in the game room. I'll call — "

She broke off as a wheelchair shot around a corner and rolled to a stop in front of them. A thin old man peered at Abby through thick glasses.

"You play chess, kiddo?" he demanded.

Abby shook her head.

He turned to Hannah. "How about you, missy?"

The woman behind the desk laughed. "Mr. Bonner, I was just going to call you. These people came to see you, but not to play games. They want to talk."

The old man looked down at the miniature chess board balanced on his knees. "The last good game I had was two months ago," he said mournfully. "Ted Palmer was pretty good. But not as good as me."

"Mr. Palmer died," the woman whispered behind her hand.

Len Bonner sighed. "What d'you want to talk about?"

"You tell him, Abby," Hannah urged.

Abby explained. "We're trying to find out about some people called Erlandson. They used to live here in Essex, and we thought you might have known them."

The old man nodded. " 'Course I knew 'em. They was customers of mine for a lot of years. I was their gardener. Nice people — always paid up and no arguments. Had a big place just west of town. Mrs. Erlandson used to say it was all they wanted — a nice quiet life in the middle of a beautiful garden."

Behind the thick glasses the old man's eyes seemed to be peering back into another world. "That was what they had," he said. "A quiet life and a beautiful garden. At least, it was a quiet life until that girl moved in. Then it weren't so peaceful anymore."

Chapter Nine

Len Bonner's Story

"What girl?" Abby and Hannah asked together. David leaned forward, interested in spite of himself.

"You ladies better sit down if you want to hear the whole story," the old man said. "Plenty of chairs here for everybody." He waited until Abby and Hannah were seated on either side of David. Then he positioned his wheelchair in front of them and began to talk.

"The girl I was talkin' about — Joan Hatfield was her name — she came to work for the Erlandsons in the spring. I remember that day well, you bet I do! I warned Mrs. Erlandson she was makin' a mistake. Too bad she didn't listen to me."

"Why was it a mistake?" Abby asked.

" 'Cause that whole Hatfield family was troublemakers, that's why. Her father was a thief and her brothers, too. Seemed as if the police was always after one Hatfield or another. But Mrs. Erlandson said none of that was Joan's fault and she deserved a chance. Besides, she was the only person who answered the ad they put in the paper. She didn't know the first thing about housekeepin', but Mrs. Erlandson said she'd teach her, and Mister said it was all right with him so . . ." Len Bonner shrugged. "So they had to find out for themselves."

"They must have been very kind people," Hannah said encouragingly.

"Oh, they was," Len agreed. "Too kind, I'd say. At first the girl got along okay. She used to come out to the garden when I was workin' and brag about how good she was at her job. Said she loved all the pretty things in the house. Trouble was, after a while them pretty things started disappearin'. Pieces of china and silver, a little painting, a perfume bottle, stuff like that. The Erlandsons called in the police finally, and they questioned everybody who'd been near the house — me included. But it was clear from the first that Joan was the one. She got real upset when the police talked to her, and when they said they'd be back the next day with more questions she started cryin' and carryin' on awful. I was out at the end of the garden, but I could hear her yellin' that she didn't want to go to jail and Mrs. Erlandson tryin' to calm her down."

"I don't think that was fair!" Abby exclaimed. "They shouldn't have blamed Joan just because her father and brothers stole things."

"Oh, she was guilty, all right." Len Bonner's eyes gleamed. "And it was that very night that the Erlandsons' grand house burned to the ground. The old folks slept on the first floor, so they got out pretty quick. But the girl's bedroom was upstairs, and she didn't make it. The police figured she set the fire herself and was trapped before she could escape."

There was a horrified silence. "Why?" Abby quavered. "Why would she burn down the house?"

"The police said maybe she planned to run downstairs and wake up the Erlandsons. She might have thought if she saved their lives they'd be so grateful they wouldn't press

charges against her for stealing. Or else, she
was so mad that she just decided to get even.
One or 'nother, it didn't work out the way she
wanted, that's for sure."

The old man looked at each of his listeners,
seeming pleased with the effect of his story,
but puzzled, too. "What's all that matter now,
anyway?" he asked. "Why do you young folks
want to know about Joan Hatfield?"

"We have a music box that was supposed to
have belonged to the Erlandsons," Hannah explained. "But if their house burned to the
ground — "

"What's this music box look like?"

Hannah described the little white chest of
drawers with blue trim, and Len Bonner nodded. "Yep, that was theirs, all right. It was one
of the things that was stolen. The reason I
know is because I was right there when the
insurance people found it — that music box
and all the other things that'd gone missin'.
They was in a little room up over the garage."
He paused, remembering. "They wasn't hidden,
understand. They was just set around the room
in a kind of circle so that the person who put
them there could admire them. Had to be Joan

Hatfield. I guess she liked 'em so much she wanted to pretend they was her own.

"I remember, the Erlandsons felt real bad when they saw that room. Even after what she'd done to 'em, they said they was sorry for Joan and knew she hadn't meant to be bad. They arranged for her to be buried in the cemetery behind their church out on Nicholson Road."

"I know that church," Abby said solemnly. "It's on our road, just before you get to town."

"That's the one," the old man agreed. "The Erlandsons paid for a headstone for her and everything. And then they moved east somewhere. Seems as if everyone I knew back in them days is dead or moved away. You're the first visitors I've had in years." He smiled at them wistfully. "Anything else I can tell you about?"

"Did Joan Hatfield wear anything special when she was working for the Erlandsons?" Abby asked. "Something white?"

The old man narrowed his eyes. "Just wore her regular clothes, near as I can remember. Except when Mrs. Erlandson had one of her fancy garden parties, of course. Then she had

Joan fixed up in a black apron-thing and a little white cap. The girl loved dressing up, I could tell. The cap and the apron made her feel important, I s'pose. . . . Anything else? I've got lots of time."

Hannah stood up. "We just want to thank you very much," she said, sounding dazed. "You've really helped us, Mr. Bonner."

David spoke for the first time. "I can play chess," he said.

Len Bonner's mouth dropped open. "You mean it?"

"We can play right now, if you want to. We aren't going home for a while." David looked at Hannah. "You're going to stores and stuff, right?"

"And the tearoom," Hannah said.

David made a face. "I'll meet you at the bus stop."

"All right," Hannah agreed, a little breathlessly. "Three o'clock." She and Abby watched as Len Bonner whirled his wheelchair around and, with a grin of pure delight, led David down the hall.

"You know, your brother is a very nice person," Hannah said softly, as she and Abby went outside into the late-morning sunshine. "I'm proud of him."

Abby thought about it. "I bet he didn't want to give you a chance to say I-told-you-so," she said. "Now he knows there really is a ghost in a white cap, just like you told us."

"Even so," Hannah said. "I don't think that's the reason he offered to play chess with Mr. Bonner."

Abby remembered the old man's wistful expression when he said all of his friends were gone. She remembered his glowing smile as he and David headed off to play chess.

"Well, I'm proud of him, too," she admitted. "It's just that . . ."

Oh, well, she thought, they could always say I-told-you-so later, when they met David at the bus.

Chapter Ten

"You'd Better Watch Out!"

"What are we going to do?" Abby asked as they started down the street toward the town center. She felt weird. Playing detective was exciting, but now, as she thought over what Mr. Bonner had told them, she almost wished she hadn't called Aunt Sarah. It was one thing to wonder whether your house was haunted. It was something else to be sure.

"First we're going to the tearoom," Hannah replied. "Maybe we'll think more clearly after we've eaten."

So Hannah was feeling weird, too. Her face had a closed-off look, as if her thoughts were a thousand miles away.

"I'm going to have a grilled-cheese sandwich and chocolate pie," Abby said when they turned into the Magic Teapot. Chocolate always made her feel better.

Hannah nodded. All through lunch she was even quieter than usual, and afterward, at the library, she sat and looked out a window while Abby chose a half-dozen mysteries. It wasn't until they reached the bus stop and found David already waiting for them that she lost her faraway look.

"Well, how was the chess game?" she asked. "Did you enjoy it?"

"Cool!" David looked pleased. "Mr. Bonner showed me some good moves. We're going to play again."

"Did he say anything more about Joan Hatfield?" Abby asked anxiously. The soothing effect of the chocolate pie was wearing off, and she was starting to worry again.

David grinned. "Said she had a wicked temper. I told him about your ghost, and he really laughed. He said ghost-talk was a lot of nonsense, but if the ghost of Joan Hatfield really was hanging around, you'd better watch out!"

"She's not just *our* ghost," Abby interrupted. "She's your ghost, too." It was as close as she dared come to saying I-told-you-so, herself.

"No way!" David retorted. "I'm not going to
start believing that stuff just because some
people called Erlandson had a maid who wore
a white cap. But I'll tell you one thing — if I
thought there really was a ghost dropping in
every night to listen to her music box, I'd toss
the stupid box in the garbage. Or throw it out
the car window! I wouldn't just moon around
waiting for her to show up."

Abby felt a wave of relief. Of course! As
usual, David had the answer.

But Hannah shook her head. "No," she said
gravely. "Throwing it away won't do at all."

"Why not?" David demanded. "Give it to me,
if you don't want to do it. I'll take it to the pond
and toss it in."

At that moment the big blue bus chugged
around the corner and gasped to a stop in front
of them. Hannah waited to answer until they
were settled in the long backseat and the bus
was on its way again.

"You haven't seen Joan Hatfield's face,
David," she said. "If you had, you'd know why
the music box can't be destroyed. Sometimes
she looks so sad that I feel sorry for her, but

most of the time she's furious. At first she'd appear, all of a sudden, in front of the dressing table, and stare at the music box for a while, and then she'd turn around and glare at me. That was bad enough, but since I packed the box away in the closet she looks really wild. Sometimes the music box starts to play, buried under all those blankets, as if her will is so strong she can start it without being near it."

Abby shivered. "You're brave, Hannah. I wouldn't have blamed you if you hadn't come back last Sunday."

Hannah shook her head. "I'm *not* brave, and you know it. But this is the first real job I've had. It's the first time in my life that I've been on my own. I *can't* fail at this! If I do, I might be afraid to try again — ever. My aunt would rather I'd just stay home with her," she added unhappily.

"But knowing the ghost would be waiting for you..." Abby tried to imagine what that must have been like. "How could you make yourself come back to that?"

"The ghost would have returned anyway. And she might have come to you, Abby. Or to

David. I couldn't bear to think of it. . . ." Hannah cleared her throat and continued in her flat voice. "David, think about what Mr. Bonner told us. Think what that girl did when she was angry."

David turned pale. "Ghosts can't burn down houses," he said uncertainly.

"How do you know? If she can make a music box start to play, maybe she can tip a candle. . . ."

Or make a wind strong enough to blow down a hanging basket! Abby remembered the day Aunt Sarah's box had arrived.

"So what can we do?" Abby wondered. "Oh, I wish Aunt Sarah had never sent it to me!"

"Somehow," Hannah answered, "we have to give the music box to Joan, so that she understands that it's hers forever."

"Give it to her!" Abby exclaimed. "We can't give it to her. She's dead!"

"Dead and buried," Hannah agreed. "But not resting peacefully, poor girl. I've been thinking about it ever since we left Mr. Bonner, and I think I know what to do. I think if she had this one pretty thing in her grave with her — "

"This is the creepiest conversation I've ever

heard!" David exploded. "You're talking crazy!"

Abby gasped, "Oh, Hannah, no!"

Hannah sat up straight and clasped her hands tightly in her lap.

"Yes," she said firmly. "Wait and see."

Chapter Eleven

Caught in the Middle

David braced his knees as the bus rounded a curve. "You wouldn't dare!" he scoffed. "People can't go around digging up graves."

"I didn't say I was going to dig up her grave." Hannah sounded shocked. "I just want to find where Joan Hatfield's buried and leave the music box there for her."

"But somebody else might come along and take it," Abby objected. "And then the ghost will haunt *them*!"

"Oh, boy!" David rolled his eyes. "Now you're both doing it! What a pair of flakes!"

Hannah ignored him. "Friday evening when your father takes me to the station, I'll have the music box and a trowel in my suitcase. As soon as he drops me off at the station, I'll take the bus to the churchyard. Or if there isn't any bus, I'll walk. It isn't so very far."

"And then what?" David jeered. "What happens when you get to the cemetery?"

"I'll dig a hole right next to Joan Hatfield's grave and bury the music box," Hannah told him. "And then I'll hurry back to the station. There's a second train at eight-fifteen."

Abby was amazed. Could this be timid Hannah talking? How could she even think of going to a cemetery all alone to bury the music box?

Hannah answered the unspoken question. "If we don't give it back to Joan, I'm afraid of what she might do. All that anger ..." She paused and then continued, a little shakily. "After all, thousands of years ago people were buried with their favorite jewelry and food and — all kinds of things."

"Thousands of years ago people did lots of weird stuff," David retorted. "Listen, it's okay for people to tell ghost stories for fun, I s'pose, as long as they don't believe them. But you can't *believe* in ghosts. It isn't scientific!"

Abby stared out the window, trying not to listen. When the bus stopped, she was the first one out.

"Abby! What's your hurry?" Hannah rushed to catch up. "Are you all right?"

"Sure," Abby said, but she had never been more confused. Her brother was disgusted, and she knew he was disgusted with her as well as with Hannah. But how could he *not* believe in the ghost of Joan Hatfield? Hannah wouldn't lie about seeing her, and Mr. Bonner hadn't been lying, either. The ghost in the white cap had to be real.

She walked faster, not wanting to see David's scornful expression.

Thursday and Friday dragged by. Hannah didn't mention her plan again, but Abby thought about it all the time. At night she lay awake, straining to hear the music box, and hearing instead a hundred creaks and whispers she'd never worried about before. During the day she tried to read, but the words blurred before her tired eyes. When she tried to work on the shoe box house, her fingers moved clumsily.

"I noticed a croquet set out in the garage," Hannah remarked after lunch on Friday. "Will somebody teach me how to play?"

David turned away. "I'm busy," he muttered.

"I'll teach you," Abby offered. Croquet was something they could do outside, together.

Strangely, it didn't help much to get out of the house. The sky was gray, and mist rose from the meadow. Abby set up the wickets and explained the rules, but she kept peeking over her shoulder at the upstairs windows. Hannah's room was at the back. It was hard to forget, even for a moment, that Joan Hatfield's ghost might be up there watching them.

Hannah kept looking over her shoulder, too.

It was a relief when the family car turned in to the yard soon after six. Abby's mother was carrying a pizza carton when she came up the walk.

"For you and David," she called gaily. "Dad and I are meeting the Johnsons in Essex for an early dinner right after we drop Hannah at the train station. Are you ready to go, Hannah?"

Hannah hung her croquet mallet on the little wire rack and started to scoop up the balls.

"I'm packed," she said stiffly. "My suitcase is in the front hall." She picked up the rack and carried it to the garage. Abby followed with the balls.

"That girl is certainly an odd one," Abby heard her father say in a low voice. "If anybody said 'Boo,' she'd jump right out of her shoes!"

When the car backed out of the driveway a half hour later, Abby stood on the front porch and waved until the headlights were swallowed in the fog. Then she wandered back into the house. David was just taking the pizza out of the warming oven.

"I don't want any," Abby told him. "I'm not hungry."

"Since when aren't you hungry for pizza?" David eyed her curiously. "If you're worrying about Hannah's so-called plan, forget it. That was just a lot of silly talk."

"I don't think it was silly," Abby said. "I think she meant it."

David helped himself to a slice of pizza. "Not in a million years. That whole ghost business is a fairy tale. Hannah's the kind of person who has to make up something, if there isn't anything real she can worry about. If she *did* believe in ghosts, she'd never actually go to a cemetery. Not scaredy-cat Hannah! . . . Are you sure you don't want some pizza?"

Abby shook her head. "I'm going upstairs," she said.

What she wanted to do was to find out whether Hannah had taken the music box with her. That meant going into Hannah's bedroom, opening the closet door, and poking around under the blankets stored on the back shelf. Abby held her breath while she searched. But when she was back in the hall, with the bedroom door closed tight behind her, she had her answer.

Hannah had taken the music box. She was going to the cemetery.

Abby's stomach churned. She felt hot and shivery at the same time. Why had she looked? Now that it was too late, she wished she had just listened to David — David who was always right.

Except this time. This time he was wrong.

Downstairs the television set blared, which meant David had carried the pizza into the den. Abby stopped in her own room long enough to write a note, and then she tiptoed down the steps.

The light streaming from the den was inviting, and the television show sounded like fun.

Abby swallowed hard and tiptoed out to the kitchen. She read her note once more — *I'll be back soon. I'm going to help Hannah.* — and propped it against the bouquet of wildflowers on top of the table.

Then, quickly, before she could change her mind, she slipped out into the foggy twilight.

Chapter Twelve

Scared to Death

The garage was full of shadows, but Abby didn't dare turn on a light. Carefully, she made her way to the shelf of gardening tools at the back. One of the trowels was missing, but an old one, with a loose handle, was still in its place. She dropped it in her bike basket and wheeled the bike down the driveway.

She'd pedaled along Nicholson Road hundreds of times, but never in weather like this. The fog cut off the view on either side and hung like a curtain across the road itself. The only sound was the hiss of her bike wheels on the blacktop.

No one in the whole world — not her parents, not David, not Hannah — knew where she was at this moment. Abby's heart thumped fiercely at the thought of it. If they did know, they would certainly tell her to turn around and go home.

She squinted into the gray curtain, searching for something familiar. Once in a while a flicker of light shone through the fog from one of the few houses scattered along the road. She began counting the crossroads, stopping at each one in case a car might suddenly appear.

When she passed the fifth crossing, she knew the church was not far ahead. On sunny days it always reminded her of a picture postcard with its neat white steeple pointing toward the sky. She and Theresa had explored the cemetery behind it more than once, searching for the oldest stones and the ones with little lambs carved on them.

This evening, though, when the church finally loomed up in the mist, it looked lonely and forbidding. Abby turned into the parking lot and propped her bike against the pole that marked the entrance. Now what? she wondered. If Hannah had caught a bus at the station, it was possible that she was already in the cemetery searching for Joan Hatfield's grave.

"Hannah? It's me, Abby!" Her voice sounded peculiar in the fog.

"Hannah!"

There was no answer, but something rustled in a tree near the road. Abby clutched the handles of her bike so tightly that her fingers ached. I can still leave, she reminded herself. If I leave now, no one will ever know I came this far and was too scared to stay.

And Hannah will have to find the grave and bury the music box all by herself.

With a sigh, Abby let go of the bike and peered down the road. She could barely make out the curve that marked the outskirts of Essex.

"Hurry, Hannah!" she whispered. But the black ribbon of road remained empty.

Behind her, something rustled in the tree again, and then a dark shape swooped across the parking lot. Just an owl, Abby told herself, swallowing hard. Owls liked hunting in the dark. Maybe they liked fog, too.

At last, when she thought she couldn't bear to wait there alone another minute, a figure appeared at the curve. At first the person seemed too tall to be Hannah, but as it drew

closer Abby could see the small suitcase in the
walker's hand. Another few steps and she rec-
ognized Hannah's long stride and the shoulder
bag that bounced against her hip.

"HANNAH!"

She raced up the road and threw her arms
around her friend, almost knocking her over.
Hannah screamed and dropped her suitcase.

"Oh, Abby!" she gasped. "What are you doing
here? You're supposed to be at home with
David. Does he know where you are?"

Abby shook her head. She was so glad to
see Hannah that she didn't mind being scolded.
"He's watching television. We can do it — bury
the music box — and I'll be home again before
he even notices I'm gone. All his favorite pro-
grams are on Friday night."

Hannah frowned. "Your mother would be furious," she worried. But then she seized Abby's
hand and picked up the suitcase. "Come on,"
she said. "Let's get it over with."

Back in the parking lot, Abby took the battered trowel from her bike basket and they
made their way across the gravel to the rear
of the church.

A low iron fence marked the edge of the

cemetery. Hannah stopped long enough to dig a flashlight out of her shoulder bag, and then she stepped awkwardly over the fence.

Abby followed. "The gravestones close to the church are real old," she whispered. "The new ones are in the back, in front of a row of tall, skinny trees."

"Yew trees, probably," Hannah said. "Joan Hatfield died fifteen years ago, so her grave is probably somewhere in the middle." She moved ahead, pointing the flashlight beam from side to side.

There were lots of trees dotting the cemetery, maples and oaks whose branches reached up into the fog. Abby hoped there weren't any more owls nearby. She was sure she'd faint if an owl — or even a sparrow — suddenly darted over their heads.

But what happened next was much worse than seeing an owl — so much worse that she froze in her tracks.

The music box began to play.

For a moment, Abby was sure the sound was only in her head. Then she heard Hannah gasp. The suitcase dropped with a thump.

"Look!" The flashlight beam, trembling

wildly, picked out a name and dates on the stone in front of them.

JOAN HATFIELD

1963–1980

Hannah knelt and opened the suitcase. She took out the music box and set it close to the headstone.

"Close the drawers!" Abby begged. "Make it stop playing."

"They *are* closed," Hannah said hoarsely. "They're closed tight. Dig, Abby! Hurry!"

Abby crouched and tried to drive her trowel into the earth next to the headstone.

"It's hard!" she exclaimed. "Like digging into a rock!" She tried again, and the trowel's loose handle twisted in her sweating hands. If only the music box would stop playing!

"Keep working," Hannah whispered. She was having more success with her digging. "Don't stop!"

Abby forced the trowel a little way into the ground, and this time the handle broke off completely. She rocked back on her heels and peered over her shoulder, not wanting to look but unable to stop herself.

The fog had begun to thin a little. Around the trees and the taller gravestones, mist still clung, silver-tinted in the glow of the moon. Abby looked toward the back of the cemetery and gave a little wail of terror. The tall thin yew trees were still topped with fog, but something was moving behind them. A shadowy figure drifted out into the moonlight and stopped.

"Hannah!" Abby's voice cracked. "Hannah, look!"

The shadow moved again. The face of the figure was still hidden, but its white cap gleamed in the moonlight.

Abby clutched Hannah's arm. "What'll we do?"

She'd heard of people being scared to death, but this was the first time Abby believed it could really happen.

Chapter Thirteen

The Ghost, at Last

"Don't look at her!" Hannah ordered. "Just dig!" She was working furiously, grunting with effort.

Abby turned back to the shallow hole. It was easy to say "Don't look," but impossible to do. She shoved the broken trowel into the ground with one hand and brushed away dirt with the other. And all the time, she kept peeking over her shoulder.

"She's coming closer, Hannah!" Wisps of fog floated around the eerie figure. Gradually, its face became clear — the face of a young girl made ugly by rage.

"Hannah, she doesn't understand why we're here. She doesn't know we're giving the music box to her. She must think" — Abby could hardly say the words — "She must think we're digging up her grave!"

"ABBY!"

The angry shout came from the parking lot and was followed by running footsteps. Abby turned back in time to see David leap over the iron fence. He looked around uncertainly to find where the music was coming from. Then, dodging between the headstones, he raced toward them.

"Wait'll I tell Mom and Dad you sneaked out! Of all the dumb things — " He broke off with a kind of croak and skidded to a stop.

"Who — who's that?" His mouth fell open as he stared at the figure shimmering in the moonlight.

Hannah reached up and gripped his arm. "Come on, David," she urged. "As long as you're here, help us!"

Abby gasped with pain as the edge of the trowel bit into her fingers. "Give me that!" David said hoarsely. He snatched the broken trowel and began to dig.

Abby stood up on trembling legs. David —

cool, smart David — was as scared as she and Hannah were. Somehow, that was the most terrifying fact of all. She wanted to run and run and never stop running.

The ghost drifted closer, the hatred in her eyes blazing through the mist that floated around her. Abby couldn't guess what would happen if the phantom came close enough to touch them, but she knew it would be terrible. Joan Hatfield hated them enough to kill them all.

The little white chest lay at Abby's feet, its music swelling now to a kind of tinny thunder. Abby edged away from the din, then stopped. A single word, even louder than the music, hung in the air:

"MINE!"

Abby shuddered. "We know," she quavered. "We know you want the music box."

The ghost turned her furious glare from the two diggers to Abby. Her eyes narrowed, and she stretched out her arms with fingers curled.

Abby forced herself to take one step forward, then another. "We want you to have the music box to keep," she said. "Honest! That's why we came. We're burying it here, where no one can have it but you."

The outstretched hands were only a foot from Abby's face.

"We're *sorry* about what happened to you," Abby choked out the words. "We know how much you want the music box. We want you to have it."

The ghost moved still closer. Fingers, pale and cold as moonlight, brushed across Abby's face.

The music box stopped playing.

"Abby, come back!" Hannah sounded far away. "The box is buried! Come back!"

Abby couldn't move. She closed her eyes, and when she opened them, the ghost had retreated into the mist. The phantom's arms were at her sides, and her face was as peaceful as the silver fog that closed around her.

"Abby!" David roared. "Come on!"

With an effort, Abby turned. David and Hannah were still on their knees, watching her with awestruck expressions. For a moment the three of them stared at each other. Then Hannah scrambled to her feet.

"Thank goodness that's over," she said in her flat, prim voice. "I have a train to catch." She took a deep breath and picked up the overnight case. And then, they were all running, hand in hand, across the cemetery to the fence and the parking lot beyond.

Chapter Fourteen

"I'll Be Okay."

"I'm going to walk back to town," Hannah said, when they'd caught their breath. "I have time, and I'd rather not wait around here for the bus."

David looked stunned, as if he couldn't believe what had just happened. "We can go to the station with you," he offered. As he said it, he glanced over his shoulder at the cemetery.

Hannah shook her head. "You'd better both go home where you belong." She surprised David then with a hug, before he could move away, and then she hugged Abby, hard. "You are a really amazing girl, Abby," she said. "Absolutely amazing! I believe you are the bravest person I've ever known."

She turned and strode swiftly down the road

toward Essex, her shoulder bag bouncing against her hip. Abby and David watched until she rounded the curve. Then they returned to the parking lot for their bikes.

"Go ahead," David muttered as they swung out onto the highway. "Say I-told-you-so. What are you waiting for?"

Abby shook her head.

"Then just tell me why you did it," he demanded, beginning to sound more like himself. "How could you walk right up to that — that *thing* — and talk to it? I wouldn't have done it — not in a million years." He looked back toward the cemetery again and shuddered.

Abby felt her face grow warm. "I wanted to stop her from coming closer," she explained. "I didn't think about it. I just did it. And you don't have to worry about her following us. She isn't angry anymore — I could tell."

It felt strange to be reassuring her big brother; usually she was the one who needed comforting. Maybe it meant that she was becoming a different Abby. After all, she had stood up to a ghost and hadn't run away. And she was the bravest person Hannah had ever known.

"Well, don't go getting a big head about it," David warned. "You'd better ride ahead, so I can keep an eye on you."

Abby shrugged and pedaled faster. What a story she'd have to tell when Theresa finally came home ... a story about an angry ghost, and what she — none other than Abby Tolson — had done to protect her brother and her friend!

"You don't have to worry about me," she shouted over her shoulder as she skimmed down the road. "I'll be okay."